Teacher

HUGH PINE
and Something Else

"There we are," Mr. McTosh said. "That's what I wanted to see. Look, Hugh, our Earth."

Hugh looked at the huge globe turning slowly. He saw the green land of the continents, the deep blue of all the oceans, and their thousands of islands, the golden deserts, the snowy mountains.

Mr. McTosh pointed things out. "That's where we live." His finger came down. "And that's where we are right now. And all the rest is where we haven't been so far."

"And outside?" Hugh asked.

"The universe, the stars, other Earths maybe."

"With people?" Hugh asked.

"Maybe."

"With porcupines?" Hugh whispered.

Hugh Pine

and Something Else

Janwillem van de Wetering

Illustrated by Lynn Munsinger

Beech Tree Books • New York

Library of Congress Cataloging-in-Publication Data

Van de Wetering, Janwillem, date
  Hugh Pine and something else.

  Summary: Hugh Pine, a porcupine, takes his first
vacation when he accompanies his human friend,
Mr. McTosh, to Brooklyn, New York.
  [1. Porcupines—Fiction. 2. Vacations—Fiction.
3. Friendship—Fiction. 4. Brooklyn (New York, N.Y.)—
Fiction] I. Munsinger, Lynn, ill. II. Title.
PZ7.V2852Hum 1989   [Fic]   88–35801

Printed in the United States of America

First Beech Tree Edition, 1992.

ISBN 0-688-11800-3

2 4 6 8 10 9 7 5 3 1

Hugh Pine
and Something Else

Chapter 1

IF YOU GO all the way north and a bit east, until you just about fall out of the country, you come to a hill that overlooks the sea. On the hill you'll see a pretty little house. Mr. McTosh lives there. When he looks out of his front window he sees the blue Bay of Sorry, and when he looks out of his back window he sees the town of Rotworth peeking through the woods. Rotworth is only a small town with just a few gray <u>weath</u>ered buildings, including the post office, where Mr. McTosh sells stamps. He likes being the postmaster of Rotworth, but he also likes his vacation starting up, and that was today.

Right now he's having dinner with his friend Hugh

Pine. Some people think Mr. McTosh and Hugh Pine are brothers because they both have gray whiskers and they're both a bit short. They also both wear long coats and red floppy hats — not now, of course, because they're in the house. Hugh Pine is shorter, but he is really quite tall.

You see, Mr. McTosh is five foot small and he's a man, and Hugh Pine is four foot tall and he's a porcupine, a very big porcupine who lives in the Sorry Woods, on the top branch of a big white pine.

Mr. McTosh and Hugh Pine have known each other for many years. Hugh Pine can walk upright, and he wears his red hat so that the cars can see him and think he's a little old man, and he can also speak quite a bit of Human.

Mr. McTosh and Hugh Pine often go walking and boating, and they visit too. They share great meals. Mr. McTosh saves his broken ax handles and old boots for Hugh, and Hugh often picks juicy mushrooms for Mr. McTosh.

Mr. McTosh is eating a mushroom sandwich with plenty of mustard, and Hugh Pine is eating a broken ax handle with plenty of salt.

"More coffee, Hugh?"

"Yes, thank you."

"More salt?"

"Yes, please." Hugh took his time emptying the shaker into his mug. Meanwhile his tufted eyebrows moved up and down. He was thinking.

Mr. McTosh laughed. "Let's have it, Hugh. Something on your mind?"

Hugh sipped his nice strong coffee. "What's a vacation, Mr. McTosh?"

"Vacation comes in between work," Mr. McTosh said.

"Work?"

Mr. McTosh sighed. "It's difficult," he agreed. "Let's put it this way. Vacation is Something Else. No stamp selling. No drive to town every day." He waved his short arms. "Vacation is something else altogether."

"Can you do Something Else here?" Hugh asked.

"Not really," Mr. McTosh said. "I'm going away for mine. To the big city. My sister Emily lives there."

"Your sister is not like people here?"

Mr. McTosh smiled. "No, Hugh, not a bit."

"Ah," Hugh said. His bristly eyebrows kept moving. He thought he maybe understood. Something Else was very different, not the same thing at all. Something Else was exciting. The same thing was okay, of course. It's good to sit on a high branch of your own tree and look far away across the shimmering water while the sun warms your pink belly and your toes stick out in

4

the breeze and you're watching the eagle and the ra-vens soar — that's good, but he did that lots of times. He often swam in the cove between the sea-polished rocks. He liked looking for fat, golden mushrooms in the mossy grove behind the fir trees. He enjoyed play-ing with the baby fox and his pinecone collection, but none of that was Something Else.

Hugh grinned. His big orange teeth shone. Mr. Mc-Tosh knew everything and could explain it to him. Now he would finally know what it was he didn't know.

"What is Something Else, Mr. McTosh?"

Mr. McTosh sucked on his pipe. "Hmm?"

"Please?"

"It's the big, beautiful blue globe in the museum," Mr. McTosh said. "It turns, you know? Like the earth? And it's glass buildings on Fifth Avenue, higher than . . . higher than —" He pointed at the low ceiling. "Yes . . . and it's Emily's parrot. He hangs upside down and hums. It's driving down the four-lane inter-state, forever and some. Why, Hugh, what's the mat-ter?"

Hugh's eyes were big and round. His mouth was open and his paws hung down. "Huh?" Hugh asked.

Mr. McTosh patted Hugh's shoulder carefully, for all Hugh's sharp spikes were standing up. "Never mind, Hugh, you don't need to worry about any of that. You like it here. Something Else is weird stuff. Emily's cat throws things down from the shelf. She has a little Pekingese dog that yaps. You wouldn't like Something Else at all." He sat back and stared at his friend. "I can do without it too." He frowned. "Yagh! You want to smell big, black fumes from rusty buses? Eat funny food from machines? Want to wait in line for everything? Like to cut your paws on old cans on the beach?" He poked with his pipe. "I have to go all the way to the big city to see my only sister, but you have lots of relatives right here, old buddy."

Hugh's long quills rattled softly.

"Hugh?"

"Big blue globe in the museum," Hugh muttered. "Four-lane interstate. The upside-down parrot that hums."

"The four-lane interstate goes on for a thousand miles," Mr. McTosh said. "You'd be bored. And Emily's parrot screeches mostly. Bad noise. Like your squirrels. Remember how you're always complaining about the squirrels? Yuk yuk yuk? Yelling all the time? That parrot is worse."

"When are you going?" Hugh asked.

Mr. McTosh got up. "Tomorrow morning early. It's a long drive, Hugh. Should take me all day. It isn't fun to sit still that long. Be glad you can stay here."

Hugh sighed.

"Tell you what," Mr. McTosh said. "I'll drive you to your tree. Doesn't do to get too excited, Hugh. You need your rest."

Hugh slid down his chair with a thump and landed on his tail. Its short, sharp spikes at the end got stuck in the floor. "I'll just sit here," Hugh said. "I often sleep sitting on my tail. I'm quite comfortable, thank you." Hugh looked grim.

"Won't you be stuck there forever?" Mr. McTosh asked.

"Just until tomorrow," Hugh said. "I feel a little weak now, but tomorrow I can pull free."

"You want me to drop you off at your tree tomorrow morning?"

"That'll be out of your way," Hugh (who really wanted to go) said firmly. "I'll tell you what. You're right, Something Else could be very tiring, I think.

Why don't you let me help you get along with it?" Hugh smiled helpfully. "Yes?"

Mr. McTosh smiled too. "You can pull free now, Hugh — maybe that'll be more comfortable. I do have a spare bed. Why don't you stay the night so that we can leave early tomorrow morning?"

Chapter 2

Mr. McTosh smoked his pipe as he drove, and Hugh stood up and looked out of the window. It was time for his late-morning nap, but Hugh was just a little too busy right then. Cars! Hugh knew cars — they sometimes came by on the Sorry Road and he looked down on them from his tree — but there were so many of them now. He kept pointing them out. "Look at the little tiny one, ooohh, look at the huge one with the split in the middle, ooohh!"

The big truck rumbled past them on its eighteen big wheels, and the driver smiled down from his high cabin. Hugh waved. A motorcycle zipped by. The rider's beard was pushed back by the wind, his long, stiff hair streaked behind his head, and his leather clothes looked rough and worn. His bike growled as it picked up more speed. "Wow!" Hugh shouted. He touched Mr. McTosh's arm. "Did you see that?"

The rider wove through the lanes, and Mr. McTosh

had to put on his brakes a bit so as not to nudge him. "See what, Hugh?"

"A Something Else porcupine," Hugh shouted. "With the quills and the fur? Exactly like me, only different?" More motorbikers passed them, and Hugh jumped and cheered. "The Something Else Club," he shouted. "Do you think I can join?"

"I'll give that club something else," Mr. McTosh

grumbled as he braked to stay clear of the bikers, who kept cutting in front of his car, but Hugh didn't hear. Hugh gaped at the quickly disappearing taillights. He was very impressed.

Then a station wagon passed with little kids in the back, eating crispy things from brightly colored bags, grinning between puffed cheeks. Hugh slid down and rummaged about on the floor. "You already ate the ax handle," Mr. McTosh said. He looked over his shoulder. The apples on the back seat were gone too. Hugh climbed up again and felt the upholstery of the seat. "That's plastic," Mr. McTosh said. "Not too tasty." Hugh's stomach rumbled so loudly that Mr. McTosh could hear it. "Did you ever try a hamburger, Hugh?"

Hugh didn't hear too well, for another big rig was roaring by. A bamburger? Sounded great. He nodded, clapped his paws, and opened the glove compartment. "Where do you keep it, Mr. McTosh?"

"The restaurants keep it for us," Mr. McTosh said. "There's one coming up, but I'll have to get out of all this traffic. Be a good buddy and help me look for a hole."

Hugh pressed his nose against the window. A big hole came up between all the vans and trucks. "Now!" he yelled, pointing with both paws. Mr. McTosh pulled out of his lane, then began to ease out of the next one too while Hugh hollered helpfully. They got to the restaurant parking lot.

Nobody paid much attention when the two feisty little characters trundled into the fast-food place. Hugh guarded a table while Mr. McTosh stood in line. He came back carrying a loaded tray. Hugh had already done away with all the little appetizers. Mr. McTosh checked the empty half-and-half cartons, the torn-up mustard, ketchup, and relish envelopes, and

11

some ragged splinters, all that was left of a dozen wooden stir-spoons.

"Kept yourself busy, Hugh?"

"Yep," Hugh said happily, licking ketchup off his lips. "Hah!" He reached for the tray. "So those are bamburgers, hey? Can I have one, please?"

"You sure can, Hugh."

Hugh was so hungry that he just about inhaled his hamburger and a large helping of French fries. He liked the coleslaw, too, and the big carton of coffee. There was no salt, and Hugh was about to go hunting for some when a little girl, who had been watching Hugh going "Hmmmm" and "Chchchrrrr" and

"Whashwhashwhash" between bites, fetched the salt shakers from all the tables nearby and lined them up neatly around Hugh's coffee carton.

Hugh poured till his coffee almost overflowed.

"Would you two care for some ice cream?" Mr. Mc-Tosh asked Hugh and the little girl while he took the tray and all the empties away before Hugh could try those too.

"Please," Hugh said.

"Please," the little girl said. "My name is Caroline. What's yours?"

Hugh and Mr. McTosh introduced themselves.

"You should take your glove off when you shake hands," Caroline said to Hugh. Hugh looked at his paw.

"He's been sick," Mr. McTosh said.

"Yes," Hugh said. "Cold hands are bad for me."

"I'm a girl," Caroline said, showing her bare hand. "I never mind the cold. Boys are weak, aren't they?"

Mr. McTosh brought two big cones of chocolate chip and Mississippi mud mix.

Caroline watched Hugh pour a heap of salt on his ice cream. She tried a little herself. "Yuck!"

Mr. McTosh spooned the salt off for her.

Hugh swallowed the end of his cone and patted his round stomach. "Wow." He smiled. "You people have great things to eat."

Caroline looked suspiciously at Hugh's big orange teeth and furry cheeks. "Aren't you People too?"

"Come along, Hugh," Mr. McTosh said, taking his friend by the arm. He nodded at the little girl. "Bye, dear, we really must go now. There's still a long way to drive."

"Bye, Caroline," Hugh said. "And thank you for helping out with the salt."

Chapter 3

THE INTERSTATE was different now. Instead of trees on hills and clouds floating quietly above faraway fields, there was more and more traffic. All the rumbling of engines and the bright colors of the vehicles made Hugh sleepy. He wanted to watch, but his eyelids got gluey. He tried shouting again — "Ooohh, look at the nasty screamer with the blue flashy eye on top trying to jump the cute little pink car!" — but Mr. McTosh only grunted. The light was mostly gone but the dark hadn't quite come yet, and Mr. McTosh kept squinting while he found a free passage. The mysterious moment made Hugh very tired. "Look . . ." Hugh whispered, but then all his thoughts floated away.

They wafted back again when Mr. McTosh's car crossed a big bridge. There were lights everywhere, lights like a thousand Rotworths — a thousand Rotworths ahead and (when Hugh turned to look back) another thousand Rotworths behind and even more in the sky. Hugh got so excited that he forgot to speak Human. He gurgled and squeaked.

"Beg pardon?" asked Mr. McTosh.

But now there were even more lights: on boats in the river below. Hugh tried to point them out all at once and hissed so loudly that he got hiccups.

"Now now," Mr. McTosh said. "Calm down, Hugh. That's the city for you. Does it every time. Take a deep breath and hold it a while."

They got off the bridge and there were more lights ahead and big arrows pointing everywhere, but all the cars had stopped. "Now what?" Mr. McTosh said. He honked his horn.

"PYOOO!" Hugh wheezed.

"Yes?" Mr. McTosh asked.

"Can I breathe out now?" Hugh asked, breathing out all at once. "Oops. Couldn't hold it, Mr. McTosh."

"I'm sorry," Mr. McTosh said. "How are your hiccups?"

Hugh couldn't find his hiccups anymore. "What did the car say?" he asked.

Mr. McTosh laughed. "That's right, you've never heard the horn before, eh, Hugh? The car just said, 'Hurry up, we're tired.' In the city the cars sometimes have a say too."

The traffic moved up again a bit. The car got lost a

few times and honked again here and there. Hugh helped. He wound his window down and asked a man where Emily McTosh lived, but the man didn't know.

"Thirteenth Street?" Mr. McTosh asked.

"Right here around the corner," the man said. "My, don't you two look from away?"

"He looked from away himself," Hugh said when he had wound his window up again. "What was that little tail he had up front dangling off his shirt?"

"Necktie," Mr. McTosh said. "City folks look nice."

"Very nice," Hugh agreed.

The car turned. "The sea!" Hugh shouted. "Are we going to walk on the beach tomorrow? Check out the city seals?"

"Why not?" Mr. McTosh asked. "Emily walks the dog on the beach. Maybe she'll let us come along."

Mr. McTosh parked the car. Hugh got out and stood in the street. The building rose high under shiny stars. All its windows were lit up brightly. On the third floor someone was waving at them. Hugh took off his hat because he remembered that was a polite thing to do when meeting with humans. When porcupines meet they usually rattle their quills a bit, so Hugh did that too.

"Hi, Emily," Mr. McTosh shouted. He deftly caught the key she dropped down to them.

Hugh didn't know about keys but was pleased when it opened the big door ahead. He did know about stairs and hopped up on the first step. Mr. McTosh called him back. "Better take the elevator, Hugh."

The elevator was a little house with another light in it and lots of polished brass buttons to push. Mr. McTosh stubbed one of them, and the little house whooshed up. "Woohoo!" Hugh shouted. He wanted a little elevator of his own to take back to his big pine tree, but they had arrived at Emily's floor before he could tell Mr. McTosh about it.

Emily smiled from the corridor when Mr. McTosh and Hugh stepped out of the elevator. She was a short

woman in a big dress that rustled as she moved. Hugh thought she smelled very nice, and he liked her big teeth and bristly white hair.

"This here is Hugh," Mr. McTosh said.

Emily clasped her hands and bent down over Hugh. "Welcome," she said. Then she looked at Mr. McTosh. "Never knew you had a son. You might have told me, brother." She pinched Hugh's cheek. "What a strapping little fellow he is, too."

"He's my little friend," Mr. McTosh explained.

"Looks just like you when you were a little lad yourself," Emily said.

"A FRIEND!" Mr. McTosh shouted.

Emily pushed Hugh ahead of her. "Come along, nephew. You'll be wanting some hot chocolate and cookies after your long trip."

Chapter 4

Hᴜɢʜ ɪs ᴜsᴇᴅ to getting up bright and early when the sun peeks round and red over the horizon across the bay and the birds start chirping lower down in his pine tree. As soon as the light tickled his nose he jumped out of bed. Mr. McTosh was snoring a bit to himself in the far corner of the room. Otherwise it was all quiet around the apartment. Hugh pushed the door open and peeped into the living room. A bright green shape fluttered above a stick that hung in a big polished cage.

"SCREECH!" exploded the parrot.

Hugh almost fell over backward and then carefully tiptoed ahead. The parrot sat watching him from bright, beady eyes, swaying on his short orange legs. He bent forward and raised both wings. "SCREECH!"

"Good morning," Hugh said nicely. He nodded at the furious bird. "Got a good strong voice on you, sir. The bluejay birds back home couldn't outshout you ever. The jays fly about a lot. Do you do that too?"

21

"Silly," the parrot screeched harshly. "Can't you see I'm locked up?" He dropped his head to the side. "Say, how come you speak Animal? What are you doing here anyway? Get out of here, this is our place!"

Something soft and hairy had been moving about on the couch and now sat up. "That's right," it yapped shrilly. "My name is Fong. I'm a Pekingese prize-dog and I'm the boss around here." The little dog jumped on the floor but kept its distance, showing little fangs. "Better leave while you still can, stranger." Fong snarled and then barked nervously. "Yip yip YIP!" It hesitantly moved a little forward.

"Easy," Hugh said, backing away. "I'm kind of prickly, Mr. Fong. Don't jump me. You might get hurt and we wouldn't want that."

BANG! Something heavy dropped on Hugh's head. Once it bounced off to the floor Hugh saw that it was a fat book. He looked up. Above him on a shelf sneered a big cat on long legs. Its tail gestured slowly. "Meow," the cat said. "I'm the mighty Nya. This is my apartment. Leave quickly before you get kind of pricked yourself." Five sharp claws flashed out of the neat velvety paw Nya showed Hugh. The cat's big blue slanting eyes were sparkling coldly.

Fong snarled and attacked while Hugh was still looking at Nya, but porcupines aren't half as slow as

23

they're said to be. Hugh saw, smelled, and heard Fong
coming. He turned, and his short, stubby tail suddenly
stuck up from under his coat. A porcupine's tail is like
a little war club, hard and strong, with short, sharp
quills sticking up all over.

"OUCH OUCH OUCH." Fong tumbled away, sev-
eral of Hugh's spikes sticking from his flat little nose.

"I did warn you, Mr. Fong," Hugh said. "I've got
those nasty things all over me. They got barbs at the
end and they're hard to get out. Wait, I'll get help
quickly."

Hugh woke up Mr. McTosh. Mr. McTosh yawned.
"I don't really want to get up yet, Hugh. This is the
city and the city is always late."

"Please," pleaded Hugh. "Mr. Fong has my spines
up his nose and he doesn't sound happy."

"OUCH OUCH OUCH," yelled Fong from the living room.

"Oh dear," Mr. McTosh said, and wriggled his toes into his slippers. "Good thing I brought my tools."

Fong howled and squirmed, but Mr. McTosh had him firmly clasped between his knees and Hugh held on to him too. The spikes came out one by one, held by Mr. McTosh's pliers. "There," Mr. McTosh said, patting Fong kindly on the back. "That'll teach you, I trust. Hugh is very friendly, so you'd better be too."

Mr. McTosh went back to bed. Fong looked suspiciously at Hugh. The parrot was so interested that he forgot to screech and instead hung upside down in his cage, and Nya jumped down from the safety of her high shelf and sniffed at Hugh's coat. "You're not a traitor, are you?" the cat asked. "Some nasty little human who learned to speak Animal so as to spy on us better?"

"Yeh," snarled Fong, and the parrot suddenly screeched again.

"I," Hugh said, "am a porcupine. I normally live in the woods on both sides of the Sorry Road, and I learned to walk upright and wear a coat and hat so that the cars think I'm human and won't dare to run me down."

"Pretty smart," admitted Fong.

"Pretty stupid," screeched the parrot. "Why didn't you learn to fly?"

"Yes," said Nya, "or jump? You look pretty crazy in your clothes. Anyway, what are woods?"

Hugh pointed out of the window. "See that tree? Put lots of trees together." He waved at the buildings outside, and the train tracks, and the beach beyond. "So this is the city? What's life here like?"

"Good," Nya said. She licked her paw and used it to wash her ear. "I get fed and I can sleep a lot, but I can't go for walks so much lately."

"And you?" Hugh asked Fong.

"Okay, I guess," Fong said, "but I'm a dog and I should run about even more than a cat, but these days I can go only when Emily takes me shopping." Fong barked crossly. "Me, I like to roam."

"That's because you can't fly," the parrot shrieked. "I get out and fly and nobody gets at me."

"Pah," Fong said, "and what about the crows? They always chase you back."

"Only when I want to go home anyway," the parrot said. "Those silly birds don't scare me." The parrot looked at the Pekingese slyly. "Some of us here scare easily, right?"

Nya looked moodily out of the window. "We all scare easily when there's a real danger about. When

Bully the bulldog comes after me I'm lucky if I can find a tree, and then I have to sit in it all day until people come with a ladder."

"Hah hah!" the parrot shrieked. "Took her down a peg, it did. Hah hah!"

"Yeh." Fong grinned at Hugh. "You should have seen her. It rained and she shrank."

"How amusing," Nya said. "And who jumped into a garbage can to get away from the selfsame Bully? And who stank up the house? And who cried and whined when Emily made him soak in a hot tub?"

"Hah hah!" the parrot shrieked. "That's because you guys can't fly." He lifted his wings. "I just take off and soar."

"With the crows after him," Fong chortled.

"Into the window," Nya said, laughing. "And when it was closed you almost busted your silly head."

Hugh looked at the dog and the cat and the bird in turns. "What are you staring at?" the parrot yelled.

"What beautiful animals you are," Hugh said as he shuffled closer to the birdcage. "Great colors. I do like your orange legs. What a wonderful shade."

"Really?" the parrot asked shyly, bending down so that he could see his feet.

"And you," Hugh told Fong. "That silky hair. Must feel great. You've got good colors, too. Like the mink

27

that lives on the shore of Pretty Pond. He's the most beautiful animal we have around." Hugh moved a bit closer to the Pekingese and gingerly put out a paw to feel Fong's hair. "But you look even better."

Fong forgot all about the pain in his nose. He smiled. "I told you," he yapped proudly. "I won a prize."

Nya stretched and purred. "And what about me? I'm a Sealpoint Siamese. Quite rare, you know. I was born and raised in a penthouse on Fifth Avenue."

#6 "Good name," Hugh said. "Now I know what you keep reminding me of. A seal, of course."

"And what is a seal?" Nya purred haughtily. "Hmmm?"

"Graceful and sleek," Hugh said, "with the softest of furs. Acrobats of the rocks and the water. One of them was good enough to teach me how to swim."

"I can fly," the parrot said softly.

Nobody heard the bird. Hugh laughed. "Seals are smart enough to be happy. They frolic a lot."

"Watch this," Nya said. She jumped and danced on the polished oak floor, rolled over on the thick carpet — a flick of her long, muscular tail brought her instantly on her dainty feet again — and pranced off without a care in the world, suddenly somersaulted, climbed a curtain, reached her shelf, dived back to the floor. She tripped around Hugh. "How's that for a good frolic?"

"Absolutely perfect," Hugh said.

Fong threw and caught a ball. Hugh said that was perfect too.

It was the parrot's turn. Everybody backed off, expecting the parrot to start screeching again, but the bird hummed softly instead, half raised his wings, ruffled his feathers so that he suddenly looked twice as big, held on to his bar with his strong toes and swung around it twice, then sang a little song, in a soft croaky voice, while he swayed, winking sleepily. Then he did screech after all, and bowed and clicked his curved beak.

"Hey," Hugh whispered, pressing both his paws on his mouth. "Wow, good show indeed!"

"I perform better at night," the parrot said. "Before breakfast I'm too stiff."

"Breakfast," Hugh said. "I always wondered what city breakfast is like."

"Seeds?" the parrot asked. "I can throw some from my dish. I got sunflower today, they're best."

"Half a sardine in peanut oil?" Nya offered.

"Crustchowder?" Fong suggested.

Hugh had quite a bit of everything. He thanked his hosts.

"Now what do you want to do?" Nya asked.

"Think things over," Hugh said, and went back to bed.

Chapter 5

"MORE PANCAKES?" Emily asked. "More bagels-rolls-biscuits-muffins-croissants?"

"Brrrppp," Mr. McTosh said, moving a little away from the table and easing his suspenders a tad. "Excuse me. No, thank you, dear."

"Hugh?" Emily asked. "More eggs anystyle? You haven't had poached yet. Care to try?"

"Brrrppp," Hugh said, and tried to catch a button that jumped off his coat. "No, thank you, Miss Emily. Very nice."

Emily sewed on the button while Mr. McTosh washed up and Hugh dried.

Hugh checked the kitchen shelf when he was done. "We're out of salt," he said.

"Yes," Emily said. "You can do some shopping. Take Fong along. He needs a walk."

Fong yapped and scratched at the door. Nya purred and rubbed her long body against Emily's ankles. The parrot flapped his wings and hooted in his cage.

"Yes, yes," Emily said and opened a window. Nya jumped into a tree. "Careful, dear," Emily said, letting the parrot out too. "Beware the nasty crows. Do come back at once when they bother you."

In the elevator Fong yapped at Hugh. "Bully is out there, waiting. Put a few quills into him for me, will you, Hugh? Bully thinks he rules the street. Thanks to him I can't go out alone."

Mr. McTosh squatted down and scratched Fong's head. "What is it, little friend?"

"Bully is a coward," yapped Fong. "He never shows up when Emily is around. Watch for him, Hugh. I'll tell you when I see him lurking about."

"What's with the dog?" Mr. McTosh asked Hugh. "Got himself all nervous, has he?"

Hugh didn't have time to answer as the elevator thumped to a stop. Mr. McTosh read Emily's shopping list. "Look at this," he said. "We'd better hurry, Hugh. This might take all day."

They walked down the street. There were some big buildings neatly filled up with apartments, but Hugh saw regular houses too, with gardens up front, just like the ones in the street behind the Rotworth post office. There were fluffed-up cats and shampooed and brushed dogs in some of the gardens.

"Look out!" they all shouted. "Bully is hiding behind his hedge again."

Fong pressed himself between Mr. McTosh and Hugh. "Bully's a killer," Fong whispered.

Bully sat in a field of weeds in front of a rough-looking house. He looked pretty strong and squat. There were scars all over his blotched skin, and both his ears looked as if they'd been ripped off and sewn back again. His big fangs stood out, and he drooled down his slobbery lower lip. His short legs trembled as if he were ready to jump straight through the hedge.

"Hello there," Hugh said. "Isn't it going to be a nice day today?"

"Khrrrwuf?" asked Bully. He seemed surprised.

34

"Nice doggie," Mr. McTosh said. "Out to take the sun, old chum?"

Bully's bit of a tail wagged.

Mr. McTosh, Hugh, and Fong walked on. "Killer, eh?" Hugh asked.

"Bah," snarled Fong. "That's because he thinks you're human. Lick up to big guys like you folks, bite down on little fellers like me. If it had just been me he would have jumped through the hole in the hedge and made me flee for my life. Why don't you go back and whack him with your tail?"

"He can't be all bad," Hugh said, looking back at the old dog staring at them, still shaking his stump.

Nya jumped down from a branch of the big tree that reached up to Emily's apartment. "Oh, Bully is all bad, all right. Don't let him bamboozle you with his cute doggie act, Hugh. It's his fault none of us housecats and dogs can play in Thirteenth Street anymore. Get him good, Hugh."

"Won't that make him badder?" Hugh asked.

"He can't get worse," yapped Fong.

"Right," snarled Nya. "Get him before he gets you."

"That's the rule," yapped Fong.

"Of Thirteenth Street," snarled Nya. She wandered off.

Mr. McTosh found the grocery store. Fong couldn't get in. "You have to tie him up to one of the hooks outside, sir," a saleslady said to Hugh.

"Hugh'll have to tie himself up too," yapped Fong.

"My, what a yappy dog you've got there, sir," the saleslady said to Hugh.

"Why don't you take Fong for a walk on the beach, Hugh," Mr. McTosh said. "I'll join you there later."

The beach was at the end of the street. "You don't want to put me on a leash, sir?" Fong asked Hugh. "I might run away and bite that nice saleslady at the store."

"If you'd walk up straight and wear a hat and coat," Hugh said, "people might think you're a little human too."

"People might think I was a little clown," Fong said. He rushed off and gamboled about on the beach.

"Nice beach," Hugh said when Fong came racing back.

"Used to be pretty dirty here," Fong said, "but then Emily came and picked up all the cans and the bottles and the other people showed up too and helped her burn the yucky stuff. Now it's better — but for Bully, of course."

Bully showed up farther along, barking at gulls. He barked at Hugh too.

"Now now," Hugh said.

Bully barked even louder and showed all his teeth. His bit of a tail and his torn ears stood up, and spittle spat out of his mouth.

"He's sorry he wagged his tail just now," yapped Fong. "He wants to show you he's a bad dog underneath."

"Get off my beach," barked Bully. "You too," he barked at Hugh Pine. "And you," Bully growled at the wheeling gulls.

Hugh Pine and Fong met Mr. McTosh at the grocery store and together they walked back to Emily's building.

"Thank you," Emily said when Mr. McTosh handed her the groceries. "I trust you left the beach as you found it, right?"

"Yes ma'am," Mr. McTosh said, "even better. Fong pointed out some garbage and Hugh and I picked it up and put it in the pails you people so kindly provided."

"Good," Emily said. "We take good care of our bit of nature here. Can't have strangers come and mess it all up."

"We got some salt for the bamburgers," Hugh said.

Emily laughed. "Right. Time for lunch!"

Chapter 6

MR. MCTOSH WANTED to take his nap and the parrot wanted to screech, so Hugh went over to ask the bird to please pipe down just a little bit.

"I always screech after lunch," said the parrot.

"Ever tried humming instead?" asked Hugh.

"It isn't humming time," the parrot said.

Hugh hummed. "Hmm. Hmm."

The parrot opened his beak to screech again when Hugh, comfortable with his tail stuck solidly in Emily's linoleum floor, began to sway, very slowly, in time with the humming. "Hmm. Hum. Hmm. Hum."

The parrot swayed a bit too.

Hugh tapped his foot. The parrot tapped a claw. Softly. "Bonk. Tick. Bonk. Tick."

"Hmm-mmmm. HUM. Hmm."

"Yap, yap," Fong said sleepily. "Yap, yap."

Nya stretched on her shelf and meowed musically. Emily sat on the rocking chair and began to knit.

The ticking of her knitting needles fitted in most beautifully.

The music got slower. Still slower.

Mr. McTosh began to snore in the next room. The parrot fell asleep on his bar, leaning over, one claw up, between taps. Hugh, halfway through a long "hum," snoozed away. Nya and Fong had rolled over and slept on their backs, paws far to their sides, mouths wide open. Even Emily dozed off.

They all woke up for tea. And chocolate cookies. Chocolate cookies and salt for Hugh.

"TV?" Emily asked.

Hugh was excited. He didn't have TV in his tree. Mr. McTosh didn't have one either yet. Hugh had seen it only once, when he peeked through a fence in Rotworth.

Fong explained. "Those are bad guys. They lose."

The bad guys fell off their horses.

The winning good guys shouted "Yip" and "Yay."

"See that fat bad guy?" asked Nya. "Doesn't he look just like Bully?"

The fat Bully look-alike bad guy fell off his horse.

"He lost," Hugh said. He waved. "Yip!" He waved some more. "Yay!"

"Bad guys lose only on TV," Nya said. "When they're for real they always win."

"We're real good guys," Fong said, "and we can't even play in our own street."

"We can't even fly above our own street," the parrot screeched. "Just look at this feather." The feather was all torn and crumpled. "The crows were after me again. They've got a nest up in the tree across the road. They think I want their eggs. Who wants eggs? I just want to fly about."

"I know some crows," Hugh said. "They live in my woods, in a tree a mile away. They sometimes visit. Crows tell good jokes."

"These crows live in my tree," the parrot screeched. "That's far too close."

"You can climb trees," Nya said to Hugh. "Is your tree higher than ours?"

"Much higher," Hugh said.

"You think you could climb our tree and beat up those bad guys?" the parrot screeched.

"If they stayed put," Hugh said. "But it wouldn't help. If I go back home they'll still be here."

Fong was tapping his tail on the floor. "Hugh?"

"Yes, Fong?"

"You could beat up Bully, couldn't you?"

"Probably," Hugh said. "I've never heard of any animal beating up a porcupine from the Sorry Woods."

"Nobody beats you up, Hugh," purred Nya. "But nobody." She stroked one of Hugh's long quills. "How sharp. How nice. Nobody beats up our big, strong porcupine."

"You got to do something, Hugh," Fong yapped. "You're our hero now. We've got this nice street and we can't even play in it. It's for the other fellows too, all the cats and the dogs and the birds of Thirteenth Street." Fong snarled. "You can do it, Hugh, you're bigger."

"Be badder than the bad guys," the parrot squeaked.

43

"That'll teach bad Bully and the crows once and for all."

"Yess," purred Nya, pushing her soft cheek against Hugh's paw.

Hugh muttered to himself.

"What was that, dear?" Nya purred.

"Something Else," Hugh muttered. "That's what I'll do, Something Else."

"Something else what, dear?" Nya asked.

"Something Else," Hugh promised. "Something Else once and for all."

Chapter 7

Hugh was up early again and had all his breakfasts. Then he watched trains rushing up and down between the apartment building and the beach. "That's the subway," Emily said.

"Sub?" asked Hugh.

"Under," said Emily. "Under the ground."

"But they're above the ground."

"Farther along they dive under," Emily said, "and there they stay. There's no room for them otherwise, you see. They have to stick to their tunnels." She turned to Mr. McTosh. "Brother, why don't you show my nephew around a bit today? Give him a bit of a view from the high building. Show him the museum, too."

"Good," Mr. McTosh said. "But Hugh's my friend, not my son."

"That's right," Emily said. "I keep forgetting. He does so resemble you."

Mr. McTosh and Hugh walked to the station. They had to wait for a bit. There were a lot of little old ladies on the platform with sharp umbrellas that they waved about. Hugh smiled at them.

"Yes?" a little old lady asked.

"Good morning," Hugh said, and smiled some more.

"Good morning, is it?" the little old lady asked. "Okay, so it is. You still can't have my seat."

"Are you a member of the committee?" Hugh asked.

"Yes," she said. The train arrived and she rushed in. She sat down quickly. All the other little old ladies sat down quickly too.

Mr. McTosh stood next to Hugh. "What committee was that, Hugh?" Mr. McTosh asked.

"The Porcupine Committee," Hugh said. "It often comes to see me. The committee porcupines make rules, and they never give up their seats."

The train went into a long, dark tunnel. It stopped. All the lights went out.

"Oh dear," Mr. McTosh said.

"I hope the train doesn't live here," Hugh said. "If it does, it may rest a while. It must be tiring to race about so much."

"You could be right, Hugh," Mr. McTosh said a good while later, but just then the train shivered, coughed, rumbled, and got going.

Every time the train stopped, Mr. McTosh and Hugh got ready to jump out, but the stations were wrong. Then suddenly one was right. They rushed off the train before the doors could slam shut again.

"Fyoo," Mr. McTosh sighed. "Now to find the building. That shouldn't be too hard, for Emily says it's practically the tallest building in town."

First they had to get out of the station. Hugh looked at the escalator. "I know stairs," he said, "but those ones don't stand still."

"That's right," said Mr. McTosh. "We hop on here and get off at the top. Saves climbing."

47

But Hugh wanted to look at the other stairs — the ones coming down. "They go right into the floor!" he exclaimed. "What happens to the people?"

"Not to worry," said Mr. McTosh. "Hop on and hop off. It's safe as houses. You'll see."

Hugh wondered why someone would say "safe as houses." "Safe as trees" seemed much more sensible. But he got on and stood right next to Mr. McTosh. "The first part was easy," he said to himself. He watched Mr. McTosh's feet, and when Mr. McTosh stepped, Hugh stepped too. It felt funny to stand on a place that wasn't moving again.

"Can you walk *down* those stairs?" Hugh asked.

"No!" said Mr. McTosh firmly. "Come along."

A man with a cap and a badge waited for them in the high building and led the way. There was another elevator-room again that zoomed up and up and up. Hugh held on to his stomach. It seemed that the parrot's pecan nuts, Fong's cowhide bone, Nya's fillet of eel, and Emily's triple-salted pancakes kept trailing at least a hundred feet below. Finally they all caught up just as Mr. McTosh and Hugh arrived at the top.

"We're in heaven, Hugh," Mr. McTosh said when the guide took them to a balcony surrounding a tall spire. "Take a good look. Now you're as high as our soaring eagles back home."

48

The view was enormous. Hugh danced around the spire, which reached up for another hundred feet in the blue sky. Hugh pointed. "Can I climb that branch too?"

"Better not," Mr. McTosh said. "You might break it."

Hugh didn't mind. Wasn't this Something Else again? He looked at the little dots far below that were cars and the tinier little dots that were people. He thought that if he were down there he would be so small he wouldn't be able to see himself. This was Something Else again indeed. He could see ships on the sea and on the rivers, a helicopter zooming around with people in it, staring. Hugh could see so far he thought he saw woods.

Hugh waved his floppy red hat in case there were any porcupines in that faraway forest.

They still had to see the museum.

"Better get down, Hugh," Mr. McTosh said. "We don't want to miss dinner."

"Lunch?" Hugh asked.

"Lunch coming straight up."

"Lemon or cream with the tea, sir?" the waitress asked.

"Both, please," Hugh said.

"Why not?" The waitress laughed. "One salted bamburger, one curdled tea."

The tea moved about and looked a bit murky, but
Hugh liked it fine. "Yech," the waitress said when she
came to check the table. "I'm sorry, sir. Just for that
you get a bamburger on the house."

They rode the subway again but stayed away from
the escalators. Hugh said he wouldn't mind trying
again. "Some other time," Mr. McTosh said, "maybe.
Steps are better, Hugh. Give you a bit of movement."

"What's THAT?" Hugh asked in the museum, nearly
falling over backward as he <u>craned his</u> neck. "Is that
a lizard? It's taller than the tree I live in."

"A dinosaur, Hugh," explained Mr. McTosh. "They aren't around anymore."

"Something Else," Hugh said with a sigh. There were other lizards too, and he stared at them all. There was a whale. "Like in the Sorry Bay?" Hugh asked.

Mr. McTosh nodded. "We saw one once, Hugh, but you saw only his head. This is the whole caboodle."

The whale was even bigger than the lizard who

could take Hugh from the top of his tree. Hugh kept shaking his head.

"There we are," Mr. McTosh said. "That's what I wanted to see. Look, Hugh, our Earth."

Hugh looked at the huge globe turning slowly. He saw the green land of the continents, the deep blue of all the oceans, and their thousands of islands, the golden deserts, the snowy mountains.

Mr. McTosh pointed things out. "That's where we live." His finger came down. "And that's where we are right now. And all the rest is where we haven't been so far."

"And outside?" Hugh asked.

"The universe, the stars, other Earths maybe."

"With people?" Hugh asked.

"Maybe."

"With porcupines?" Hugh whispered.

Mr. McTosh laughed. "Very likely."

"And outside the universe?"

Mr. McTosh shrugged. "I don't know."

"Does anybody know?"

Mr. McTosh sighed. "Not that I know of."

They were both quiet during the long ride back to Emily's apartment.

"Mr. McTosh?" Hugh asked, just before they arrived.

"Yes, Hugh?"

"Outside the universe, will Something Else be there?"

Mr. McTosh got up and guided Hugh to the door. "Yes," he said on the platform. "I reckon it had better be there too."

Chapter 8

THAT EVENING Mr. McTosh went to bed early and Emily fell asleep watching the bad guys fall off their horses again. Hugh sat around and told Nya, Fong, and the parrot about all his adventures of the day.

"Nice," the parrot shrieked. "I'd like to see the world too, but the crows won't let me even fly around the roof."

"Great stuff," yapped Fong, "but I'd be happy if I could only cross the street."

"And nobody in the city caught on that you're really one of us," hissed Nya. "You're supersmart, Hugh. You'd better help us out."

Hugh sat up most of the night and stared out of the window, but he didn't see the splendid full moon above the calm waters on the other side of the rails, where even through the magic hours the trains kept trundling about.

Finally the sun came up, and Hugh slipped into his coat and hat. He looked in the kitchen and located a piece of pie, which he wrapped in a paper bag. He went down to the ground floor and wedged a pebble between the big glass doors so that he'd be able to get back in.

Bully had spread his bulky body across the sidewalk in front of the building but sat up when he saw Hugh.

"Morning," Hugh said. "Care for some pie?"

Bully sat up, wagged his stump, presented a paw.

Hugh shook the paw, said, "Good doggie," and handed out a fair piece of pie. He watched Bully eat, nodded, and walked on.

The crows flew about the big tree, mindful of their nest filled with eggs.

"Hey," Hugh shouted. "Morning. Like some nice pie?" The crows dived and caught the pieces neatly, cackling their thanks.

"Good birds," Hugh said, and smiled at Bully too. "You guys hang out here for a bit and I'll see if I can get you some more of that nice pie, maybe." He smiled, turned, and went back into the building.

"We watched you," Fong yapped when Hugh walked into the living room. "We want you to get them, not feed them. So you're a traitor after all."

"Why didn't you whop the crows when they came down to you?" the parrot shrieked. "You could easily have pulled their nasty tails. Whose friend are you?"

"Why are you holding out on us?" hissed Nya.

Hugh grinned. Then he suddenly looked fierce. He crooked his paw. "Come here."

The parrot couldn't leave his cage, so Hugh sat close to him on a stool. Nya and Fong crouched at his feet.

"Listen," whispered Hugh. "Whisper whisper whisper," went Hugh.

"Har har," laughed Fong.

"Hee hee," snickered Nya.

"Great," screeched the parrot. "That'll do for Bully okay but what about my bad guys, the crows?"

"Whisper whisper whisper," went Hugh.

"Right," shrieked the parrot. "Hreeh hreeh."

Chapter 9

"Now," Hugh said. He let the parrot out of his cage and opened the window. "You know what to do?"

"Sure," the parrot screeched.

"Don't do it before your time," Hugh said. "Good luck."

Fong was so excited that he sat up and waved his paws. Hugh laughed. "Sitting pretty? Good boy." He patted the little dog on the head. "Come along, Fong, you're supposed to show me the rear door and a place near it where I can hide my coat and hat."

"This will be fun," Nya said. "See you outside." She stalked off quietly.

Five minutes later Bully, sunning himself on the sidewalk, wondering whether he would turn over now or maybe wait a while, saw suspicious movements out of the corner of his eye. It couldn't be. But maybe it was.

Bully sat up. Well, whaddyaknow? One silly intruding spoiled housecat and one stupid trespassing lady's lapdog. On Bully's sidewalk. Whaddyaknow?

"Hey," Bully said. He didn't really feel like being up and about. He would just talk to these little fellers. Briefly explain what was what. Straighten the spineless ignorants out. Make sure this sort of thing wouldn't happen again, or else.

"Hey," Bully said.

"Oh, hello, Bully," Nya purred. "You look great today. Nice to see you again."

"Hi, Bully," Fong yapped. "It has been too long, been keeping good?" He kept his head to the side. "My, aren't you the biggest best bulliest bad boffo ever to buffalo about on this great turf!"

Bully sat up and tried to scratch both his ears at the same time. Surely he wasn't hearing right. What was with these clowns?

"Watch it," hissed Nya.

Bully began to growl deep in his wide chest. That cat went too far.

"Behind you," Fong yapped.

Bully grinned wickedly. He had been a street fighter all his life. Old trick. Behind him indeed. If he looked round, these two jokers would try for his throat.

"Behind you, behind you!" Fong danced and pointed. "There, watch it, Bully."

Nya was staring too, and not at Bully. Nya's back curved, her eyes were like slits, and she was spitting with fury.

Okay. Bully would look behind him for just a second. Just to make sure. There would be nothing there, of course.

He looked. He forgot to growl. What the . . . what the . . . what was that huge, dark, bristly thing prancing on the pavement, standing up, squatting

down, swaying, and oh, what . . . what . . . *what*
was that terrible noise? That rattling and heavy
wheezy breathing and that devilish hoarse voice say-
ing "WOOOOH, WHOOOOO"?

"The Beast!" hissed Nya.

"The Beast!" yapped Fong.

Nya jumped and Fong rushed toward the Beast,
each on one side of Bully. Bully just sat there. He
couldn't believe what his own eyes told him. Big
orange teeth? Nobody had orange teeth. A blunt head,

wobbling up and down, bristling with spikes? A short, flat, wide swishy tail, with more of those deadly things wickedly glinting in the sun? What was happening today, a nice, quiet sunny day on Thirteenth Street, Bully's turf?

"Wrah," the Beast grunted. It stood on its hind legs and raised its great paws. "WRAAAHHH!"

Fong and Nya attacked, but the Beast only stepped back a little. "Yap yap, hiss hiss hiss, MEOOW, YAP, wrah-wrah-WRAAHH." Sharp nails flashed, big teeth glinted. Fong changed into a hairy little ball of deadly fury, Nya became a long streak of spitting rage, but the Beast stepped this way and that way and just kept getting closer to Bully bit by bit.

I'm too old for this, Bully thought, but never mind. Bad guys are brave. He took a deep breath and charged, straight at the Beast's ferocious face.

The Beast stopped, stepped aside so that Bully couldn't make contact. Fong and Nya regrouped and came in again, Fong slowly closing in from the left, Nya slinking up from the right, making room for Bully to stomp heavily forward in the middle. The Beast roared. His enemies kept coming. The Beast turned.

The Beast dropped down and humped off toward the street's big tree. Was he giving up? Trying to flee? He wasn't hurrying, exactly. The Beast just calmly approached the big tree, and once he got to it he slowly climbed up, securing strongholds by pushing his strong curved nails in the bark.

The crows, who were watching the fight from above, got very nervous. The Beast was getting very close to their nest. Did it eat eggs? They circled the Beast, flapped their wings, yelled at it to go away.

The Beast climbed on.

"Help," cackled the crows.

66

Nya helped. The courageous cat followed the Beast, but the Beast didn't mind at all.

"HELP!" cackled the crows.

The situation was, clearly, hopeless. The huge Beast just kept climbing, closer and closer to the nest filled with the crows' precious eggs. The crows were frightened off by the Beast's big orange fangs, and Nya couldn't get to it because of the evil swishing spiked tail, and . . . oh dear — what was that green flash?

The green flash shrieked down from the apartment building. Its long, wide wings gave it perfect aim. Between brilliant feathers shone a dangerously sharp curved beak. Its wicked claws pointed at the Beast's head. Its earsplitting war cry tore at the Beast's ears. The Beast couldn't stand the parrot's terrifying onslaught. The Beast slid down the big tree's trunk, hit the sidewalk with a resounding thump, shook its head, rattled its tail, and humped off quickly.

Everybody was so happy that nobody saw where the Beast humped off to. It just disappeared.

"Hurrah!" cackled the crows. "Thank you, parrot. Hurrah, hurrah!"

"Well," the parrot said, "what could I do? I'm a bird too. When fellow birds are in trouble the least I can do is help."

Bully and Fong were grinning at each other. "Showed that big oaf what sort of rules we stick to here," Bully said. "Hey, pardner?"

"Wouldn't know what do without some good bully dogs around," Nya said. "I mean, after all, this is our street, and when beasts lurk around we do have to police it."

"You're a pretty good cop yourself," Bully said. "Wow, I liked the way you got into that tree. The parrot helped out a lot but you were scaring the Beast good too."

"You think so?" Nya asked. "I thought it was mostly you."

"I did something," Bully admitted, "but without you guys I never had a chance."

Fong looked around. "The Beast may come back."

"Oh, that's all right," Bully said, "as long as us pardners stick together."

"Morning, fellows," Hugh Pine said, coming around the building, nicely dressed in his long coat and red hat. "What was going on here? I thought I heard something."

Bully growled, Fong yapped, Nya meowed, the crows cackled, and the parrot screeched, all at the same time.

"I see," Hugh said. "Well, whatever it was went

away. That's nice. You guys should be able to enjoy the street by yourselves. All together of course. I'm glad everybody won. Especially as it is time to share some breakfasts."

Chapter 10

"I LIKE SOMETHING ELSE," Hugh said on the way back, "but I like more of the same too. It's nice almost being back again."

"Yes," Mr. McTosh said, holding on to the wheel. "Might make a last stop for a salted bamburger, though."

Hugh nodded thoughtfully. "Will the little girl Caroline be there? The little girl who brings over all the salt shakers?"

Mr. McTosh shook his head. "I don't think so, Hugh. You don't see the same little girls much in road restaurants."

"In that case, I'll pass, thank you," Hugh said. He was watching fewer cars and more trees and sniffing the air. He thought he could smell Home.

Mr. McTosh laughed. "You know, I was watching you guys this morning. That was something else all

71

right. You've got that Bully and the crows wrapped up good."

"We're good friends now," Hugh said. "I'll miss them all."

Mr. McTosh nodded. "You could just see them again. Emily said she might come over next summer if I didn't mind putting up with her animals too." He touched Hugh's arm. "Would you care to help?"

"Yay!" shouted Hugh. "I can show them around. Bully and I could hike in the woods. Look for mushrooms and berries maybe. I'm sure he'd like that stew you make sometimes."

"I thought Bully was a bad guy," said Mr. McTosh.

Hugh grinned. "Bad guys should have good times too. He can meet the seal, and Fong can play with the baby fox's pinecone collection, and Nya can nap in my tree and the parrot and the crows can fly to the island in the bay."

Mr. McTosh smiled. "And screech and cackle all they like. My, didn't those birds stir up a racket!"

They drove on. Hugh was thinking so much about his new friends that he had to close his eyes. He began to breathe deeply.

"Here we are," Mr. McTosh said, nudging Hugh. "There's your tree, Hugh, waiting for you."

"Hmm," Hugh said sleepily. "So soon? Yes. Hmm. See you. Bye."

He got out of the car, shuffled to the big pine tree, embraced the trunk, and climbed up very slowly. "Hmm," he said. "Thank you, Mr. McTosh. I'm glad you showed me Something Else."

"Bye, Hugh," Mr. McTosh said, looking up until Hugh finally reached the highest branch. "Sleep well."

"You too," Hugh Pine called back, after he had got himself settled comfortably on his branch.

Mr. McTosh drove home. He kept chuckling to himself. "Something Else indeed," he muttered. "That might be a very good other name for good old little Hugh Pine himself."